Wendy and Brian and the Hurt Puppy

Wendy and Brian and the Hurt Puppy

By

Edna O. Menzies

MOODY PRESS
CHICAGO

©1978 by
THE MOODY BIBLE INSTITUTE
OF CHICAGO

Third Printing, 1981

Library of Congress Cataloging in Publication Data

Menzies, Edna O.
  Wendy and Brian and the hurt puppy.

  SUMMARY: Despite their parent's disinterest, nine-year-old Wendy
Tompson and her ten-year-old brother determine to grow like Jesus
Christ and to attend Camp Good Hope in the summer.
  [1. Christian life—Fiction. 2. Camping—Fiction]
I. Title.
PZ7.M532Wl   [Fic]   78-2640
ISBN 0-8024-1937-2

Printed in the United States of America

To
all the faithful
staff at The Mailbox Club
who helped in the
preparation of the manuscript

Contents

1

The Torn List

Wendy closed the door quietly and tiptoed over to the teacher's desk. Now, if she could only find that list! It had on it all the names of those who were to sing at the retirement home next week.

"Oh, I hope my name is on it," Wendy whispered to herself. Quickly, she began to hunt among the papers on the desk. At last she saw the list under the edge of the blotter. Wendy pulled it out and read the names eagerly. Her name was not on it!

"Mean old teacher," Wendy muttered, tears stinging her eyes. "She knows Granny is in that home. And I especially wanted to go and sing for her." With an angry jerk, Wendy tore the list in half and pushed it deep into the trash can. Then she rushed out of the room.

"Wendy, stop!"

Wendy turned slowly. Her teacher, Miss Wilson, was just coming out of the office. "What are you doing here, Wendy?" she asked.

Wendy's heart pounded as she said, "I—I— went back to put a book away."

"Well, run on home now. You know you shouldn't be here," Miss Wilson said with a frown. Her heels clicked impatiently as she hurried off down the hall.

With a sigh of relief, Wendy left the school and ran toward home. Her brother, Brian, was swinging on the gate, watching for her. "Bet you had to stay in," he said with a grin.

"I did not," Wendy answered, trying to push past him. "Is Mother home?"

"No," Brian said, scowling. "And Mother and Daddy are going away tomorrow as usual. They will be gone all weekend. This time you are to stay with cousin Janice. But I have to go to dull Uncle Bill's again."

Wendy looked at her brother's unhappy face. He was nearly ten, just a year older than she was. He liked to play ball with his friends on Saturdays. But of course he could not do that when he went to stay with Uncle Bill, who lived in the next town. It did not seem fair that he had to spend so much of his time at Uncle Bill's gloomy home. *If only Granny still lived here,* Wendy thought sadly. *Then Brian and I wouldn't have to stay with relatives so often.*

The next day the hours passed swiftly as Wendy and Janice played together. Janice was a few months older than Wendy. She had light brown hair that she kept pushing back from her face, and her blue eyes sparkled with mischief. She was fun to be with, because she laughed a lot and she could always think of some new game to play.

When they were getting ready for bed that night, Janice said, "Tomorrow we will go to Sunday school and church. It's really great! You will like it a lot."

Wendy was not sure about that. But the next morning as they entered the classroom she saw what Janice meant. The teacher was young and cheerful. The other girls seemed happy and eager to begin.

"Today we are going to learn about a wonderful place called heaven," the teacher began. "Heaven is God's home. God lives there. His Son, the Lord Jesus, lives there too. It is a very beautiful place, and it is full of joy. The reason it is such a happy place is that nothing bad or mean can ever get into heaven. There aren't any sick people there. And no one ever dies."

Wendy nudged Janice. "It's not a true story," she whispered. "Everybody dies. You know they do."

Janice shook her head. Then she held up her hand and asked, "Teacher, this is a true story, isn't it?"

"Yes," the teacher smiled as she answered. "It is all written in God's Book, the Bible. Best of all, we can go and live in heaven too."

"How?" Wendy asked the question without thinking.

"It's like this," the teacher explained. "We are glad when our name is written on a special honor roll at school. But the most important place to have our name written is in the Lamb's book of life. That book is in heaven. It belongs to the Lord Jesus. He is the Lamb. All who have their names written in His book will go to heaven. Jesus will write your name there if you take Him as your Savior."

The teacher held up a large sheet of paper with a Bible verse printed on it. "This verse is found in the last book of the Bible—the Book of Revelation. It says, 'And there shall in no wise enter into it any thing that defileth, neither whatsoever worketh abomination, or maketh a lie: but they which are written in the Lamb's book of life.' That's Revelation 21:27. It means that all who do bad things and tell lies cannot go to heaven. Only those who have their names written in the Lamb's book of life can enter heaven."

While the rest of the class read the verse aloud, Wendy sat very still. She had suddenly remembered the torn list and the lie she had told Miss Wilson. *It's no use,* Wendy thought. *I didn't get my name on the list at school. And now Jesus won't put my name in His book of life, either.* Wendy was so troubled that she did not hear another word the teacher said.

After church Wendy's father came to her cousin's house and hurried her into the car.

"Janice," Wendy whispered as she was saying goodbye. "Can a person who has told a lie ever get his name in Jesus' book?"

"Yes," Janice answered quickly. "If they confess it and say they are sorry, Jesus will—" Just then Wendy's father started the car, and Janice's words were blown away as the car sprang forward.

Wendy leaned back with a sigh. *Did Janice mean I would have to tell Miss Wilson about that lie?* she wondered. *I could* never *do that.* Her head was full of questions. She glanced at her father, but his mouth was set in a grim line. *He doesn't like to answer questions anyway,* she thought. *Only Granny ever has time to answer questions. I've just* got *to see her. And I* will *go with that group next Friday—somehow!"*

2

The New Puppy

Wendy did not want to go to school on Monday. But she could not think of an excuse to stay home, so she went. All during the day she watched Miss Wilson and wondered if she had missed the list yet. Finally, just before school let out, Miss Wilson said, "Did anyone see a pink slip of paper? It was a list of those who are to sing at the retirement home on Friday."

As Miss Wilson paused, Wendy felt as if everyone were looking at her. Her heart began to pound. It sounded so loud in her own ears that she was afraid those sitting near her could hear it too. She did not dare look up but kept her eyes on her book and scarcely breathed.

At last Miss Wilson said, "Well, I have made another list, and I want to check it. Please stand up as I call your names."

15

Even Susan Blake is going, Wendy thought crossly as a pale, thin little girl stood up. *Guess I can sing just as well as she can. And I wouldn't dress so poorly either.*

On the way home Wendy's feet dragged. Her mind was busy trying to think of a way to go with the group on Friday. Perhaps if she just went to Miss Wilson and told her how much she wanted to go with the group, Miss Wilson would let her go. But no, she remembered now that Miss Wilson had said there would be room in the cars for only fifteen students, and they already had been chosen. Wendy knew she would have to take someone's place in the cars. But how could she do that?

As she reached the house, Brian popped his head out of the garage door. "Wendy, come here," he called. "Look what I've got!" He pointed to a small puppy curled up on an old rug in the corner of the garage.

"Oh, isn't he cute!" Wendy cried, falling down beside the brown and white puppy.

"Watch out!" Brian warned. "His foot is hurt. Don't pick him up."

"Where did you get him?" Wendy asked, gently smoothing the puppy's head.

"I was coming down Bently Street." Brian's brown eyes were shining and his words tumbled out excitedly. "A car passed me. Then it slowed down. I thought they wanted to ask me a question or something. But they just opened the car window and dropped this puppy out. Then they roared away. The puppy sort of yelped and rolled over, so I ran and picked him up. I'm going to call him 'Captain.' He's mine now."

"Yes, of course," Wendy agreed. "I think 'Captain' is a nice name. Do you think he feels bad because his people didn't want him, Brian?"

Brian nodded. "I guess so. But we will show him that we want him. He will soon forget them."

Wendy laid a soft finger on the hurt paw. "Poor little Captain," she said. "I'm so glad they didn't kill you. I don't suppose dogs can get their names in Jesus' book and go to heaven."

Brian sat back on his heels and stared at Wendy. "What are you talking about?" he asked.

Wendy explained about the lesson she had heard on Sunday. "But I don't think Jesus will write my name in His book," she finished sadly.

"Why not?" Brian wanted to know.

"Oh, just because," Wendy answered. Then she said quickly, "Brian, why don't we take Captain across the park to old Mr. Warren. He might fix Captain's foot. He made Billy's cat better, remember?"

Brian grinned. "Hey! That's a good idea. Come on."

Mr. Warren welcomed them with a smile. He was a soft-spoken, kindly old man with white hair and gentle hands. The children could tell that he loved animals just by the way he held Captain and spoke to him in a quiet voice. He cheered the children up by telling them the puppy's foot was only slightly sprained.

"This pup will soon be chasing squirrels again," Mr. Warren said, chuckling. "Right now though, he wants you to comfort him. I am glad you are kind to animals. God gave them into our care, you know. But some people don't treat them very well."

Wendy moved closer. "Mr. Warren," she asked, "are dogs different from people? On the inside I mean?"

Mr. Warren nodded. "Yes, Wendy. God made the animals and the birds and the fish in the sea. But animals *are* different on the inside, because they cannot know God like we can. God made *us* with a special place in our heart. He did this so we could get to know Him and love Him. He wants us to talk to Him in prayer."

"Aw, I think God is too busy for that," Brian said, holding out his arms for Captain.

"What do you mean, son?" Mr. Warren asked quietly.

"Well—," Brian hesitated. "Most of the time our parents are too busy to bother with us. I just thought God was like that too."

Mr. Warren looked sad for a minute, then he said, "No, children. God is not too busy. He loves you both very much. He sent His Son, the Lord Jesus, to die on the cross for you. He wants you to take Jesus as your Savior. Then you can talk to Him and tell Him all your troubles."

Wendy felt a lump rise up in her throat. With all her heart she wanted to belong to Jesus and get her name in His book. If only she had not told that lie!

Brian looked thoughtful as he thanked Mr. Warren and they said goodbye. Wendy slowly followed her brother toward home. Her heart felt heavy and tears burned in her eyes. *Granny could tell me what to do,* she thought. *Perhaps Mother will take me to see Granny on Saturday.*

3

Wendy Gets Her Own Way

When Wendy and Brian reached home, Wendy pushed open the kitchen door and called, "Where are you, Mommy?"

"I'm in here," her mother answered from the living room.

Wendy stood in the living room door and took a deep breath. "Mommy," she asked, "will you please take me to see Granny on Saturday?"

Her mother sighed as she put down her empty coffee cup. Tossing aside the magazine she had been reading, she stood up, stretching lazily. Then as she looked at Wendy's tear-stained face and tangled hair, she drew her brows together in an angry frown.

"What a sight you are, Wendy!" she scolded. "I suppose you have been fighting with Brian again.

21

No, I won't take you to see Granny. She's too old to be bothered with children. Run on now and clean up."

Wendy whirled and ran up the stairs to her room. Flinging herself on the bed, she pressed her face hard into the pillow. "Granny does so want to see me," she sobbed. "I know she does. Maybe Daddy will take me. I think he would want to see his own mother once in a while. And it has been weeks and weeks now since they took Granny to the home." But as Wendy remembered how busy her father always was and how impatient he became when she asked him a question, she knew she would never have the courage to ask him. *I don't care, she thought. I will get to see Granny some way. I'll—*

Suddenly Wendy choked back her sobs and sat up. An idea had just popped into her head. Jumping up, she opened a dresser drawer and pulled out a bright red sweater. It was almost new. *I know what I'll do,* she told herself. *I'll give this sweater to Susan if she will let me go in her place. And I bet she will, too.* Carefully she folded the sweater and put it in a paper bag.

At recess time the next day Wendy called Susan

Blake aside. She explained to her what she wanted and showed her the sweater. "You can have it for keeps, Susan, if you will let me go in your place," Wendy said. "Just tell Miss Wilson that your parents don't want you to go."

Susan reached for the sweater and held it up against herself. Her pale face lit up with delight as she felt the soft warmth of the red sweater touch her arms.

"Oh, Wendy, it's so pretty. I've always wanted a red sweater. But what if the teacher phones Mother and asks why I can't go?"

Wendy thought a minute. Then she said, "Don't tell Miss Wilson until Friday morning. She will be too busy to phone then. But be sure and tell her that I am ready to go in your place."

"OK," Susan agreed. "And thanks for the beautiful sweater, Wendy."

The next two days passed slowly. Brian asked Wendy to tell him once more about the Lamb's book of life. She told him all she could remember. But when he wanted to know why she could not get her name written in it, she would not tell him.

Just before the bell rang on Friday morning, Miss Wilson hurried into the classroom. "Oh, there you are, Wendy," she said. "Susan has just told me that her parents don't want her to sing at the home today. She said you will go in her place. Is that right?"

"Yes," Wendy nodded. "I'd like to go. And I'm sure it will be all right with my mother."

"Well, if it is all right with your mother, I guess you can go," Miss Wilson said, writing Wendy's name on the list she held.

"Thank you, Miss Wilson," Wendy said in a small voice. Little prickles of excitement crept down Wendy's back. At last her name was on the list! Wendy could hardly believe it.

When the other children came crowding into the classroom, Wendy smiled at Susan and gave her a little nod. Susan's serious face broke into an answering smile as she went to her desk.

It seemed to Wendy that the hours simply crawled by, minute after slow minute. But finally it was afternoon and the group of happy children laughed and shouted as they climbed into the waiting cars and headed for the retirement home.

At the home Wendy's heart beat fast as she sang in front of the crowd of elderly people. Granny was sitting right in the first row. She looked so pleased when she saw Wendy that

Wendy could hardly keep her mind on the words she was singing.

When the program was over, Miss Wilson started the students on a tour of the building. Wendy watched for her chance. Soon she slipped unnoticed from the group and ran back to Granny.

"Oh, Granny," she cried, throwing her arms around her. "When are you coming home again?"

Granny hugged her close. "Dear little Wendy," she said softly. "I've been wanting to see you so much. How are you and Brian doing?"

Wendy brushed back her hair and smiled into Granny's eyes. "Brian is all right. He has a new puppy. His name is Captain and—"

"What about you, Wendy?" Granny's voice was kind. "How are you getting along without me?"

Wendy was quiet for a minute. Then she kneeled close to her granny and whispered, "Granny, I wanted to ask you. Why do people do bad things? Things like telling lies and getting into a temper?"

"Don't you remember the Bible story I told you, Wendy? It was about the beautiful garden that God made for Adam and Eve. He told them they could eat the fruit of every tree in the garden except one. Then Satan came and tempted them. They ate the fruit that God had told them not to eat. Adam and Eve wanted their own way. They sinned, and they passed their sinful natures on to us. Now we are all born with sin inside. That is why we do wrong things, Wendy."

"But, Granny! How can I *stop* doing bad things so I can get my name in Jesus' book?"

"Wendy!" Miss Wilson cried, hurrying up to them. "I've been looking everywhere for you. I told you all to stay together. You are a naughty girl for disobeying me, and I shall certainly have to punish you."

"Wendy and I haven't seen each other in a long time," Granny told Miss Wilson. "It was my fault for keeping her here. Please don't punish her for it."

"Well, we'll see," Miss Wilson answered.

4

Wendy Finds The Answer

As their car pulled away from the retirement home, Wendy felt sick with disappointment. If only Granny could have finished explaining things to her! Wendy thought of what Granny had said about Adam and Eve and how they had disobeyed God.

I'm just like Adam and Eve, Wendy told herself. *I wanted my own way, even though I knew it was wrong. I gave my red sweater to Susan without asking Mother, and I got Susan to tell Miss Wilson a lie. Then I disobeyed Miss Wilson by leaving the group at the Home.*

Wendy pressed her face against the car window and pretended she was looking at the houses along the street. *All I wanted to do,* she thought, *was find out how to stop doing bad things so I can get my name in Jesus' book. But Granny didn't have time to tell me. And now I don't know what to do.*

After supper Wendy went to her room. She sat on the floor and stared out the window into the back yard. Brian pounded on her door a couple of times and called her to come and play. But Wendy told him she did not want to play.

Wendy's throat ached from trying to hold back the tears and there was a big lonely feeling deep inside her. She looked up into the sky where the stars were beginning to come out.

"God," she said softly, "this is Wendy. I want to go to Your home in heaven some day because the teacher said it was such a happy place. But I don't know how to get my name in Jesus' book of life. Won't You please show me how?"

Wendy held her breath for a second as the stars twinkled silently down upon her. Then suddenly she jumped to her feet.

I know what I'll do. I'll phone Janice tomorrow and see if they will come for me on Sunday and take me to Sunday school again. And I can ask that nice teacher there what I want to know.

Maybe Brian will go too, she thought happily as she got ready for bed.

As Wendy snuggled under the covers, she felt very tired. But just before she fell asleep she murmured, "Thank You, God, for showing me what to do."

The next morning Wendy went out to the back yard where Brian was playing with Captain. "Brian," she said, "let's go to Sunday school tomorrow."

Brian tossed the ball toward the eager puppy and watched him scamper after it. Then he said, "Sure, I'd like to go. I want to find out if it's true about that book in heaven where we can get our names written."

"It *is* true," Wendy said quickly. "Just ask your teacher tomorrow and see. Come on and let's phone Janice now. We'll ask if Uncle Jim will pick us up."

As soon as Janice heard what they wanted, she called her father to the phone. He sounded pleased. He promised to come for them and to bring them home again after lunch.

When their mother came home, Wendy and Brian asked her if they could go. "Oh, I don't care," she said with a shrug. "But you will have to get yourselves ready. And don't make any noise. Your father and I are going out tonight, and we will want to sleep late tomorrow."

In Sunday school the next day, Wendy listened closely as the teacher told them that the Lord Jesus wanted everyone to go to heaven and live with Him forever. She reminded them of what a beautiful and happy place heaven was because no sin could enter there.

Wendy held up her hand. "My Granny told me that Adam and Eve sinned. And now *we* are all born with sin inside."

"Yes, that is right, Wendy." The teacher put a picture of Adam and Eve on the right side of the flannel board. Then she showed them a round piece of paper with the word *God* printed on it. She placed it on the left side of the flannel board.

"Because we have sin in us we all do wrong things. Doing wrong is sin, and sin separates us from God."

"How can I get my name in Jesus' book then, so I can go to heaven?" Wendy asked, her face troubled.

The teacher smiled as she explained, "It's like this, Wendy. God loved us too much to leave us in our sin and unhappiness. He sent His Son, the Lord Jesus, to take the punishment for our sins."

Taking up a picture of the cross, the teacher put it in the center of the board and continued. "The soldiers took Jesus out and whipped Him. They put a crown of thorns on His head. Then they nailed Him to the cross where He died. He died to pay for your sins and for mine. And now we no longer need to be separated from God."

"Do you mean that Jesus took the punishment for things we do like telling lies and disobeying?" Wendy asked.

"Yes, dear," the teacher answered. "God took all the bad things we have done and He laid them on Jesus. Now, all we need to do is to believe that Jesus died for our sins and receive Him as our Savior. The moment we do that, God forgives us of all our sins. Acts 16:31 says, 'Believe on the Lord Jesus Christ, and thou shalt be saved.' "

At last Wendy understood. "I'd like to do it right now," she said.

There was a glad light in the teacher's face as she said to the class, "Let us all close our eyes." Then she said to Wendy, "Now, Wendy, you pray and tell Jesus that you believe He died for you. Tell

Him you are sorry for your sins. Ask Him to be your Savior."

The other children were very still as Wendy prayed. Then the teacher prayed and the class was dismissed.

As Wendy was leaving, the teacher put her arm around her and said, "I hope you will come to Sunday school every Sunday, Wendy. And remember you can take all your troubles to Jesus now."

"And my name is written in His book of life," Wendy said, her eyes shining.

"Yes, indeed," the teacher agreed as she said goodbye.

On their way home in the car that afternoon, Wendy leaned close to Brian. "I've got my name in Jesus' book now," she whispered.

"You have?" Brian said. "Well, our teacher told me it was all true. He told us a lot of other good things too. And Uncle Jim told me that he would come for us every Sunday if we wanted to go. He is going to talk to Daddy about it today. If Mommy and Daddy will let us, I want to go every Sunday."

"Me, too," Wendy said.

At school the next day Wendy knew she would have to tell Miss Wilson about the lie and the torn list. "And I'll have to tell her how I got Susan to lie, too," she thought, feeling scared. Then she remembered that Jesus would help her, and she began to feel better.

Just before the last bell rang Miss Wilson said, "Some friends of mine are offering a free week of camp to five of my best students this year. You will be chosen for your effort in school and most of all for good behavior. I hope you will all do your best."

Wendy's heart sank. How could she tell Miss Wilson now? It would spoil her chance of going to that camp. Wendy stood up slowly. The other children pushed past her and rushed out the door. Wendy started to follow them. But suddenly she turned and ran back to the teacher's desk.

5

The Spoiled Notebook

"Miss Wilson," Wendy said, "I've got something to tell you."

Miss Wilson was picking up her books. "I'm sorry, Wendy," she said. "I have to go to a teacher's meeting now. Come and tell me tomorrow morning before school begins."

As Wendy reached the school gate, Susan came running up to her. She looked worried. "Wendy," she asked, "why were you talking to Miss Wilson? Has she found out about what we did?"

"I was going to tell her," Wendy said. "But she didn't have time to listen now."

"Wendy Tompson! Are you going to tell her about me, too?" Susan cried.

"I— I— was just going to tell her that on Sunday

at Sunday school I— I— asked Jesus to forgive me for the bad things I had done. And I asked Him to be my Savior. He did, too. Now I have my name in Jesus' book of life. So—"

"I don't see what all that has to do with me," Susan interrupted with an impatient toss of her head. "What are you going to tell Miss Wilson about me? That's what I want to know."

"I was just going to tell her that I was sorry for tearing up the list, and for the way I got you to let me go to the home in your place. Please understand, Susan. I have Jesus now, and I've just *got* to tell Miss Wilson that I'm sorry."

But Susan could not understand it at all. "I think you are real mean, Wendy," she said. "If you tell Miss Wilson, she won't let me be in the camp contest. And I suppose you will tell your mother about the sweater, too. Then she will make me give it back."

Wendy caught her breath. She had not thought of that. Of course she knew she would have to tell her mother about the sweater. But she did not want to take the sweater away from Susan.

"I'll beg Mommy to let you keep the sweater, Susan," she promised. "And I'll tell Miss Wilson it was all my fault about Friday. I don't think she will blame you. Please don't be mad at me, Susan," Wendy pleaded.

Susan's face was like a storm cloud. "I *am* mad at you, Wendy," she said. "And if you go and tell everything, you'll be sorry!" Quickly she turned and ran down the street.

After supper Wendy had a chance to tell her mother about the sweater. But she did not tell her. In bed, Wendy tossed and turned, trying to think what to tell Miss Wilson. At last she got up and kneeled down. "Dear Jesus," she prayed, "please help me to do what is right." Then she got back into bed and went to sleep.

The next morning Wendy found Miss Wilson waiting for her. Wendy told her all about tearing up the list and telling a lie and getting Susan to lie too. "Please don't blame Susan. It was all my fault, Miss Wilson, and I am sorry," Wendy finished.

Miss Wilson was quiet for a few moments. Then she said, "I'm sorry that you don't see your granny more often, Wendy. If I had known before, I would have let you go to see her. However, I am glad you have told me all about this now, and I will forgive you. I hope you will not do anything like this again. You can tell Susan it is all right."

"Oh, thank you, Miss Wilson," Wendy said, smil-

ing happily. "And I promise to try hard from now on."

Wendy was eager to tell Susan what Miss Wilson had said, but Susan did not come to school all day.

At home that afternoon Wendy looked for Brian. Then she saw him coming across the park with Captain close at his heels. "What have you been doing?" she asked. ·

"Getting rid of doubting Thomas," Brian answered with a grin.

Wendy looked so puzzled that Brian laughed out loud.

"Didn't your Sunday school teacher tell you about what happened when Jesus rose from the dead?" Brian asked, sitting down on the step.

Wendy sat down beside him. "She told us that Jesus came out of the grave on the third day. Lots of people saw Him. I can't remember how many."

"Five hundred at one time," Brian said. "Well, when I told some of the boys at school that Jesus had risen from the dead, they laughed at me. They said I was a sissy to believe all that. Then I began to wonder if it really was true.

"After school I went over to talk to Mr. Warren. He said I had doubts just like one of Jesus' disciples named Thomas. The other disciples told Thomas that Jesus was alive again. But Thomas didn't believe them. He said he wouldn't believe it until he put his finger into the nail prints in Jesus' hands. After a while Jesus came and He said to Thomas, 'Thomas, come and put your finger in the nail prints in My hands. Don't doubt any longer. Believe!' "

"Oh," Wendy sighed. "Thomas must have been ashamed."

"You bet he was," Brian agreed. His round, good-natured face grew serious as he continued. "And I felt ashamed too. Especially after Mr. Warren reminded me of all the things the Lord Jesus suffered so that I could be saved. It must have been terrible for Jesus to have a crown of prickly thorns pushed down on His head. And they made fun of Him and even spit on Him, Wendy." Brian's voice choked, and he was quiet for a minute or two.

Wendy was eager to hear what happened next. She knew it was something big, something really *important* to Brian. She could tell that by his voice and the way his dark eyes had been glowing while he talked. But now Wendy was sure Brian had a lump in his throat, and she knew what that felt like.

So she made herself sit very still and wait until he was ready to go on.

"Well," Brian gave a little cough to clear his throat. "I asked Mr. Warren if I could take Jesus as my Savior right then. He said I could. So I did and I *know* it is all true now. And I never want to be a doubting Thomas again."

"Oh! I'm so glad," Wendy said. "And isn't it good that Jesus is living now and He helps us when we ask Him to?" Then she told Brian about the torn list and how Jesus had helped her tell Miss Wilson.

"Whew!" Brian said. "You sure did get into a lot of trouble. And you still have to tell Mother about the sweater."

"I know," Wendy answered. "Not tonight though, 'cause Mommy and Daddy have gone out again."

The next day Wendy worked hard on her notebook. She knew that Miss Wilson would be pleased when she saw how neat it was.

Susan was not at school in the morning. After lunch Wendy came early to finish her notebook. As she entered the hall she saw Susan run out of the classroom and through the side door. "Susan, wait!" Wendy called. But Susan dashed on without turning her head.

"Maybe she forgot something," Wendy thought. She sat down and opened up her notebook. Her eyes grew wide with dismay. There, on the neat pages, were great dark smudges! There was a sinking feeling in Wendy's heart as she whispered, "Oh, what will Miss Wilson say? Will she believe me when I tell her I didn't do it?"

6

Wendy Learns To Forgive

When Miss Wilson came, Wendy showed her the notebook. "I didn't do it, Miss Wilson," Wendy said, "Honest, I didn't."

"Now, Wendy, don't tell me that," Miss Wilson said. "It must have fallen off your desk and been trampled on. You had better stay after school and do it over again."

She doesn't believe me, Wendy thought, going back to her desk. *But someone else* did *do it.* Suddenly she remembered about Susan running away from the classroom. *I bet Susan did it,* Wendy told herself angrily. *Just wait till I see her!"*

After school Wendy stayed and worked on her notebook. She felt angry and unhappy, and she kept making mistakes. At last she put down her pencil and closed her eyes. "Dear Lord Jesus," she whispered, "please help me to forgive Susan. And please help me to do my work well." Then she began to write once again.

When Wendy got home from school, she found her mother preparing supper. "Mommy," Wendy said. "I've got something to tell you. I— I— hope you won't be angry with me."

Her mother looked at her sharply. "What is it?" she asked.

Wendy started at the beginning. She told her mother everything that had happened. Then she said, "At first I wanted to see Granny because I was so lonesome for her. But when I heard about Jesus' book of life, I knew I just *had* to see Granny so she could tell me how I could get my name in Jesus' book. But she didn't have time to tell me, so I asked the teacher at Sunday school. She showed me what to do and now I have my name in Jesus' book and I love Him so much, Mommy. But I'm sorry for all the wrong things I did, and I asked Miss Wilson to forgive me. Will you forgive me, too, Mommy?" Wendy asked, tears filling her eyes. "I'm sorry, really I am."

As Wendy finished, her mother shook her head slowly. "I never thought a child of mine would do such a thing," she said. "I really should give you a whipping, Wendy. I will, too, if you don't get that sweater back here tomorrow."

"Oh, Mommy," Wendy begged. "Please, please, let Susan keep the sweater. It wouldn't be fair to take it back, since I did go in her place. I promise I'll wear my blue one all the time without grumbling."

Her mother looked at Wendy's pleading face. At last she said, "Oh, well, I suppose she had better keep it since you've given it to her. And, yes, Wendy, I'll forgive you this time." Her mother paused for a minute. Then she went on, "If you want to see Granny all that much, I guess I can take you and Brian to see her on Saturday."

"Oh, Mommy, thank you," Wendy said, smiling happily.

The next day Susan was still absent. So after school Wendy started toward Susan's home. The sky was full of dark, gray clouds. Soon a misty rain began to fall. Wendy hurried on. But in a few minutes the rain came pouring down and by the time Wendy neared Susan's house, she was wet and cold.

Wendy had never been to Susan's home before, but she knew the number of the house. It was a small house, painted an ugly dark green. The

paint was peeling off in spots here and there, and a board over the door hung loose and banged in the wind that swept around the corner of the house. The curtains in the window near the door hung limp and gray.

Wendy knocked on the door a couple of times, but no one answered. She was just turning away when she saw Susan peek through a curtain.

Wendy jerked the door open and stepped inside. "Susan," she called, "It's me, Wendy. Why didn't you answer the door?"

Susan came slowly into the room. "I suppose you came for the sweater," she said, frowning.

"No," Wendy answered as she wiped her shoes on the mat and began to unbutton her jacket.

"You'd better not take your jacket off," Susan warned. "It's cold in here and the furnace has gone out."

"Isn't there anyone else at home?" Wendy asked. She shivered as she sat down and pulled the damp jacket close around her.

"No, Mother is working," Susan answered. "Did you tell your mother about the sweater?"

"Yes," Wendy said, smiling. "You can keep the sweater, Susan. And Miss Wilson said to tell you it was all right about Friday."

"Oh, thanks." Susan's troubled face brightened for a moment. Then she looked down at the floor and was quiet.

Suddenly Wendy had an idea. "Susan," she said, "will you come to Sunday school with me on Sunday?"

Susan shook her head. "I tried going to Sunday school once. I thought it would make me good so I could go to heaven. But it was no use. I still did bad things, just like before. So I stopped going."

"But, Susan," Wendy said, "we cannot get to heaven by being good. That is why Jesus came and died on the cross. He died for your sins and for mine. Now all we need to do is to tell Him that we are truly sorry for the wrong things we have done. We must believe that He died for us and ask Him to be our Savior. And, if we ask Him, He will do it."

Susan looked as if she were going to cry. "You don't know what a mean thing I've done, Wendy. If you did—"

"Oh, yes I do," Wendy broke in. "I saw you run from the classroom. You marked up my notebook, didn't you?"

Susan nodded slowly. Two large tears ran down

her cheeks as she whispered, "Did you tell on me, Wendy?"

"No," Wendy said. "I forgive you, Susan. Jesus will forgive you, too, if you ask Him."

"Won't I have to wait and do it in church, Wendy?" Susan asked.

Wendy thought for a moment. "No, I don't think so," she said. "Because Brian took Jesus as his Savior over at Mr. Warren's place. And the teacher told me we could talk to Jesus any time we wanted to."

"Then I want to ask Him right now," Susan said. "Because I am sorry I got mad at you and spoiled your book, Wendy. And I do want to belong to Jesus so I can go to heaven."

The two girls knelt in the chilly kitchen. Susan prayed and asked the Lord Jesus to forgive her and be her Savior.

Then Wendy said good-bye and ran all the way home in the cold wind.

That night she could not go to sleep. She was still tossing and turning when her parents came to bed. "Mommy," Wendy called, "my throat hurts."

Mrs. Tompson came and felt Wendy's head. In a few minutes she came with a thermometer and took Wendy's temperature. Her voice was worried as she said to her husband, "John, you had better call the doctor. Wendy is very sick."

7

Wendy Shows The Way

For the next few days Wendy was very sick. Her head and chest ached, and her throat felt prickly and sore. Her parents often looked worried as they bent over her bed. Each day when he got home, Brian came to sit with her.

One day when he was sitting beside her, Wendy whispered to him, "Brian, I want Granny. Do you think they would let her come?"

"Sure," Brian said, getting up. "I'll tell Daddy."

It was not long before Granny came. She smoothed Wendy's hair back from her hot forehead and talked to her in a soft voice.

Wendy gave a tired sigh. "Oh, Granny, I prayed that you would come. And now you are here. God does listen to us, doesn't He?"

"Yes, Wendy," Granny answered. "Brian told me

that you both belong to Jesus now. So God is your heavenly Father and you are His child. He loves you, Wendy, and He wants you to ask Him for everything you need."

"I just needed you," Wendy said as she fell asleep.

The next afternoon Wendy's father came to sit with her while Granny was resting. "Would you like me to read to you, Wendy?" he asked.

"Yes," Wendy said. "Read to me about the Lamb's book of life where my name is written."

Mr. Tompson's face was puzzled as he looked toward the bookshelf. "What book is it in, Wendy?" he asked.

"It's in Granny's Bible there on the table," Wendy told him. "I think she left it open at the place."

Her father picked up the Bible, and after a few minutes he found the verse and read it to her. "Do you understand it, Wendy?" he asked.

"Yes," Wendy answered. "Granny explained the hard words to me. I told a lie, you know, just like the verse says. But I asked Jesus to forgive me and be my Savior. And I know He did. Now I'm not afraid to die, 'cause I know I will go to live with Jesus in heaven."

"You're not going to die," her father said quickly. "Don't think about such things, Wendy."

Wendy smiled. "But, Daddy, I *like* to think about heaven and about my name being written in Jesus' book. Is your name in it, too, Daddy?"

Mr. Tompson moved uneasily in his chair. "I guess not, Wendy. I've been too busy to think much about it," he said.

Wendy lay quiet for a while. She watched her father as he looked through the Bible, stopping now and then to read silently. He seemed to have forgotten all about her.

Wendy wondered what her daddy had been like when he was a little boy. He always looked so stern and unhappy. It was hard for Wendy to imagine her daddy chasing after a puppy like Brian did, or to think of his eyes crinkling up in fun like her brother's. Yet Granny often said that Brian was just like his father used to be.

"Daddy," Wendy said at last. "Didn't Granny take you to Sunday school when you were a little boy?"

"Yes, Wendy," her father answered, still turning over the pages of the Bible.

"Didn't you like the stories about Jesus, Daddy? And if you did, why did you stop going?"

"I don't know, Wendy," her father said thought-fully. "I suppose I thought I was too old to listen to the Bible stories. And then I got so interested in my job and making money that I didn't bother going to church anymore."

Wendy touched her father's arm. "But Daddy," she said earnestly. "Couldn't you start going with us to Sunday school again? Maybe that would show you the way to heaven and make you want to get your name in Jesus' book."

Mr. Tompson looked sad as he put the Bible back on the table. "It's been a long, long time since I went to Sunday school, Wendy. I wouldn't know what to do there." Then, as he saw Wendy's disappointed face, he leaned toward her and whispered, "Don't worry, young lady. You have shown me the way clearly enough. I'm just not ready to take it yet, that's all. But I promise to think about it. Now, it is time you went to sleep again."

A few days later Susan came to see Wendy. "Oh, Wendy," she said, "I'm so sorry you have been sick. Miss Wilson gave me your books and said I could help you catch up on your lessons. She said it was one way I could show you how sorry I was for spoiling your book."

"You told her?" Wendy said in surprise. "I'm

glad, Susan. Now she knows that I was telling her the truth."

"Yes," Susan said. "And when I told her that I had asked Jesus to come into my heart, she said she was going to let us both try for the camp contest. 'Cause she liked the way we had come and told her when we had done wrong."

"Oh, good," Wendy said. "I hope we can go together, Susan."

The girls were still working on the lessons when Granny came into the room. They told her all about what Miss Wilson had said. After a while Granny asked, "Wendy and Susan, do you think you will ever do anything wrong again?"

"We don't want to," Susan said, "but maybe—"

"Won't Jesus keep us from doing bad things?" Wendy asked.

"You are both right," Granny said. "Jesus is living in your heart now, so you won't *want* to do bad things. But sometimes you will do wrong. Just remember that Jesus is ready to forgive you. And He will help you to do what is right, if you ask Him."

"I'm going to ask Him every day," Susan said as she got up to leave.

That evening when Granny had finished reading the Bible to Wendy and Brian, Wendy said, "Granny, do you think Mommy and Daddy will ever take Jesus as their Savior?"

"Yes," Granny answered. "If we pray for them and keep showing them the way."

"I think Mommy will pretty soon," Brian said. "Because this morning when I went to the store for her she asked me why I did things without grumbling anymore. I told her it was because I had Jesus. And she said if it changed me as much as it had Wendy then she was going to find out more about it."

"And Daddy promised to think about it, too," Wendy told them. "Now, if only *you* could stay with us, Granny, everything would be just right."

"Well, I have a surprise for you," Granny said with a smile. "Your parents have arranged for me to spend every weekend with you from now on."

"Great!" Brian shouted. "No more dull Uncle Bill's."

"Oh, Granny," Wendy said. "I've got my name in Jesus' book of life. And now I'll have you, too." Her eyes were shining, and her heart was singing with happiness. Wendy was content.

8

The Contest Winners

By the next week, Wendy was feeling better and wanted to go back to school. But the doctor told her she must stay at home for another ten days. At first Wendy protested and begged her mother to let her go to school.

"No, Wendy," her mother told her. "You have been a very sick girl, and you need to get your strength back before you can go to school again. Besides, I thought you would be happy to have another week with your granny."

"Oh, is Granny staying with me? I thought she would have to go back to the home today." Wendy leaned back against the soft pillows with a smile. "It's all right, Mommy. And if Susan can bring my school work every day I guess I won't get too far behind. I just *have* to keep up with my lessons you know, because both Susan and I want to win in the camp contest. You will let me go to camp if I win, won't you, Mommy?"

Her mother pulled back a curtain and stood looking out the window as she asked, "Why do you want to go to that camp, Wendy? There are other camps closer to home where we could send you."

"But this one is a special camp, Mommy. It is called "Camp Good Hope." Isn't that a nice name? And Miss Wilson says it is a church camp, so I'm sure they will teach us more about the Bible and about Jesus. That's why I want to go. Please say yes, Mommy," Wendy coaxed.

Mrs. Tompson turned from the window and looked at Wendy thoughtfully for a minute. She seemed about to ask another question but instead gave a quick sigh and opened the door. "We'll see when the time comes," she answered. "Be a good girl now, and don't pester Granny while I am away at work."

The days soon slipped by, and when Wendy went back to school she found she was not behind in any of her work.

"I'm so glad you are my friend, Susan," Wendy said that afternoon as they left school. "I would have had a hard time catching up in my lessons if you hadn't brought them to me each day."

Susan's thin face flushed at the praise. "I wanted to do it, Wendy. 'Cause you know it was your coming to see me in all that rain that made you get sick."

"Oh, well," Wendy shrugged. "I'm better now, so forget about it. Have you asked your mother if you can go to camp if you win in the contest?"

"Not yet," Susan answered. "I'm so afraid she will say no that I keep putting off asking her."

"I think you should ask her," Wendy said. "We have been praying about it, haven't we? So even if she says you can't go, we'll just keep asking Jesus to please help her to change her mind. And He will too, if He wants you to go."

"OK," Susan agreed. "I'll ask her tonight."

When Wendy reached home, she found Brian watching for her. He looked as if he were bursting with some exciting news. But instead of telling her, he started chasing Captain around the yard and shouting, "Guess what's happened, Wendy! Guess what's happened!"

Wendy tossed her books on the step and raced after her brother. "What is it, Brian?" She grabbed

his arm and hung on as she cried, "Tell me, quick!"

Pulling away, Brian turned a handspring on the grass and then lay back panting, "G-g-guess, Wendy. See if you can guess."

"You got one hundred on your history test."

"Aw, it's something miles better than that," Brian said, sitting up. His face was bright with happiness as he went on, "Remember that day I got rid of doubting Thomas and asked Jesus to be my Savior?"

Wendy nodded as she sank down on the grass beside him. "Yes, but that was weeks ago now, and—"

"Listen," Brian interrupted, "the next day after that, I told the other kids at school all about it. Not *all* the kids, but the ones in our gang that sort of hang around together. Most of them laughed at me just like they had before. All except Randy Williams. He didn't say anything. He just looked sort of uncomfortable and walked away. But ever since then he has been real friendly to me. And do you know what he told me today?"

"What?" Wendy asked. She hugged the wriggling puppy close to her and waited eagerly.

"Randy told me that he had taken Jesus as his

Savior over a year ago, but he had been afraid to tell the other kids 'cause he knew they would make fun of him. Then after he heard what I said to them he felt so ashamed that he didn't know what to do. He kept feeling more and more miserable until he finally went to his Sunday school teacher in their church and told him all about it. His teacher helped him to pray and ask Jesus to forgive him. And today Randy told the boys that he believed the same things I did and he didn't care if they laughed at him or not."

"Did they laugh?" Wendy asked.

"Oh, a few of them did, like Micky Davis and Bunty and Crab Jenkins. But most of them just looked embarrassed and ran off to the ball game. But there's something more. Something just great."

"What is it?" Wendy asked. "Do hurry, Brian. You always take so *long* to tell anything exciting. Don't keep stopping. Just *tell* it!"

Brian laughed. "All right, Miss Impatience. When Randy and I were coming home from school, he asked me if I was going to Camp Good Hope. I told him that I thought it was just for the contest winners in your class. But he said it was for anyone, boys and girls both. The only difference is that the contest winners go free and the others have to pay their way. He said he is going and he wants me to go too."

"Oh, Brian, won't that be great if you can go!" Wendy said, delighted. "Are you going to ask Daddy?"

"You bet I am," Brian answered. "Right after supper tonight."

When supper was over, Brian waited for his chance and followed his father out into the back yard. Wendy prayed as she washed the dishes, *Dear Jesus, please let Brian go to camp too.* She knew her prayer was answered when Brian came into the kitchen, his face one big smile. He told her that their father said he would pay the camp fees but he thought that Brian should earn his own spending money.

Wendy decided she would need some spending money too, so for the next few days they both hurried home right after school. They found many little jobs they could do for the older people living in their neighborhood.

Wendy insisted that Susan try to earn some money, too, even though Susan's mother had told her she could not go to camp. "Mommy said we just don't have the money to get me the clothes I would need," Susan told Wendy sadly.

But Wendy would not give up. "I'll see if Mommy will let me give you some of my last year's things that are still nice but are just too tight for me. You are smaller than I am, so I hope they will fit you. And, Susan, keep praying. I just *know* that Jesus will get us to that camp somehow."

Susan and Wendy continued to work hard at their lessons, and Miss Wilson praised their efforts a couple of times. Some of the others in the class looked at them with envy. But Linda Sooter, who sat behind Wendy, was the only one who became really jealous. Often when the teacher was at the far side of the room, Linda would murmur just loud enough for Wendy to hear, "Teacher's pet." Wendy's face would grow hot, and sometimes anger burned in her heart.

"You should tell Miss Wilson what Linda says," Susan told Wendy when they were by themselves. "It isn't right for her to call you that. I think Miss Wilson is being fair to everybody in this contest."

"I know," Wendy answered with a sigh. "But I don't want to say anything to Miss Wilson about Linda. Linda is smart and she might even be one of the winners. And I don't think she knows Jesus,

Susan, so she needs to go to camp and learn about Him. But I'm sorry when I get angry with her in my heart."

At last the long awaited day arrived. Just before the class was dismissed, Miss Wilson took up a folded piece of paper from her desk. The room became very still, and Wendy felt a tight knot curl up in her stomach. She drew a quick, sharp breath as Miss Wilson began to speak.

"I want to congratulate the whole class," Miss Wilson said. "Most of you have improved in your work as well as in your conduct. I wish I could give many more of you free camp tickets, but I have only five and these are the names I have chosen. Please stand up as I read your name. Jim Ferguson, Susan Blake, Paul Burton, Linda Sooter, and Wendy Tompson."

9

The Golden Verse

As Miss Wilson called Wendy's name, Wendy felt glued to her seat. The room swam before her eyes as waves of happiness swept over her.

"Wendy," Miss Wilson said, "aren't you going to stand up?"

"I'm sorry, Miss Wilson," Wendy gasped, jumping to her feet. "I was so glad that I forgot to stand up."

The class laughed, and Miss Wilson smiled as she said, "I hope you will all appreciate what my friends are doing for you. And I will expect to hear a good report of each of you when camp is over."

When the class was dismissed, many of them crowded around the winners of the contest and teased them good-naturedly. They warned them about the wild animals in the bushes and told them to be careful in the water and not get drowned. Wendy noticed that Linda did not take part in the noisy chatter, but walked quickly away with her friend, Alma.

"I hope Linda won't still be mad at me when we get to camp," Wendy said to Susan as the two of them started toward Wendy's home.

"Don't worry," Susan assured her. "Linda won too, so she hasn't any reason to be jealous of you now." Susan gave a little skip of excitement as she changed the subject.

"Oh, Wendy, do you *really* think my mother will let me go to camp?"

"Yes, I do, Susan." Wendy's voice was serious. "We have been praying about it so long, you know. And then Mother told me this morning to bring you home with me and see if the things we found will fit you. She said if they did that she would take you home and ask your mother to let you go with me. My mother knows that camp wouldn't be the same to me without you, Susan."

The girls were happy to find that most of the clothes fit Susan nicely. Then Mrs. Tompson and Wendy took Susan home. After Mrs. Tompson and Mrs. Blake had a long talk together, Susan

and Wendy were overjoyed to hear Mrs. Blake say that Susan could go to camp.

The next few days were busy and exciting ones. All Wendy and Susan and Brian and Randy could talk about was camp. And on Friday morning they were all packed and waiting as the big bus stopped for them in front of the Tompson's house.

The children said a quick good-bye to their parents and climbed into the crowded bus. Everyone was talking and laughing and singing as the bus rolled along. The two-hour trip passed swiftly and, almost before they knew it, they were driving into the camp grounds.

The bus stopped in front of the large dining hall, and a counselor stood up and quieted the excited children. She told them to leave their things on the bus and go directly into the dining hall as lunch was ready for them.

"Wow! Am I hungry!" Brian exclaimed a few minutes later as he sat down to a plate piled high with good things.

"You shouldn't be after you finish all of that," Randy teased. His blue eyes were full of laughter as he added, "I bet if the camp director knew how much you eat he would have charged you extra."

"Look at your own plate, man," Brian retorted.

"If—" he stopped suddenly as the voice of Mr. Douglas, the camp director, came over the loud speaker.

Mr. Douglas told them that as soon as they finished eating, the counselors would be waiting by the buses to take them to their cabins. "When you have put your things in your cabin, I want you to come at once to the main building in the center of the grounds. Don't waste any time," he advised. "I will expect to see you there in twenty-five minutes, so you will have to hustle."

The children soon finished eating and were taken to their cabins. "Oh, Susan! I'm so glad we are in the same cabin," Wendy said, unpacking a few things swiftly and pushing her suitcase under her bed.

"So am I," Susan answered. "And isn't Miss Marion, our counselor, nice? She even gave us beds close together. Come on, we'd better run, or we'll be late."

Inside the main building the girls sat down and looked around them. They saw Brian and Randy sitting across the aisle from them. The building soon filled with boys and girls, and Mr. Douglas stood up to speak to them.

"Welcome to Camp Good Hope," Mr. Douglas

began. "I am very glad to see you all. If you are happy to be at camp, clap your hands."

The clapping started hesitatingly at first but grew louder and louder until finally Mr. Douglas had to cover his ears. Then he laughingly waved them to silence.

"Thank you," he said. "I can see we are all going to have a good time together. Now I will tell you the camp rules and what is expected of each one of you."

After explaining the rules he told them there would be points given for such things as clean cabins, good behavior, crafts, and sports. He also said that they would each be assigned a camp "buddy." "I want you to help your buddy. Be kind to him. See that he is not left out of things and that he does not feel lonely. I hope that by the time camp is over you and your buddy will be good friends."

Mr. Douglas then turned to the wall behind him and uncovered a large, framed Bible verse. "Oooh," Wendy whispered, "isn't that beautiful, Susan?"

Susan nodded. Her fascinated gaze was fixed on the golden letters that shone brilliantly against a dark red background.

At Mr. Douglas' suggestion, the children read the words in unison, pronouncing each word clearly. "That ye might walk worthy of the Lord unto all pleasing, being fruitful in every good work, and increasing in the knowledge of God. Colossians 1:10."

"That is our golden verse for camp," Mr. Douglas told them. "It means that we are to live every day in a way that will be pleasing to the Lord Jesus. First of all, we must accept Him as our Savior. Then we can please Him by doing kind deeds and by being helpful and obedient. As we study God's Word, we will learn more about the Lord Jesus and how we can grow to be more like Him each day. I want all of you to memorize this verse before you leave camp. Now, I am going to tell you who your buddy is."

"Oh," Susan whispered nervously. "I'm scared I'll get someone I don't like."

"Me, too," Wendy murmured. "I wish we didn't have to take one." She glanced toward Brian and Randy and saw them looking at each other rather doubtfully. Just then Brian turned and saw her troubled face. He smiled and motioned toward the golden verse. Wendy nodded and felt suddenly comforted. Of course Jesus would help them to love their camp buddies, no matter who they were. With all her heart, Wendy wanted to please the Lord Jesus and grow to be more like Him.

Mr. Douglas had already begun reading the names. As their names were called, the camp buddies went to the front and then went back and sat down together. Brian's name was called along with a Pete Brown.

Wendy watched in dismay as she saw a stocky, tousle-haired boy shuffle his way to the front. His jeans hung on him as if they belonged to an older brother, and he was scowling darkly as he looked at Brian. But a warm feeling rose up in Wendy's heart for her brother as she saw him reach out a friendly hand to Pete and smile at him cheerfully.

Oh, Wendy thought. *Brian is starting to grow already.* She glanced up at the golden verse once again. *Help me to grow too, Lord Jesus,* she prayed in her heart. *Help me to grow* real *fast.* Wendy could hardly wait for her name to be called.

Wendy and Brian and the Hurt Puppy

10

Stolen Money

Mr. Douglas continued calling out the names of the camp buddies. Randy's buddy was a boy named Joey Maliski. He was short and wiry with a suntanned face and a happy grin.

Suddenly Wendy gasped as she heard her name called along with a girl named Maggie Saunders. Wendy stared in disbelief as a chubby girl in a rumpled skirt and dirty sneakers made her way clumsily to the front ahead of Wendy. Maggie gave Wendy an uncertain smile as she held out her hand.

Wendy made her face smile back as she took Maggie's hot, sticky hand. As they sat down together, Wendy's thoughts tumbled about in her head. *I want to love Maggie,* she told herself. *But how can I? She isn't even clean!*

Just then Susan's name was called, and Wendy saw a pretty girl named Cheryl Tucker go up to meet Susan. Envy rose in Wendy's heart as she looked at Cheryl's lovely pink dress and bright golden curls that shone in the sunlight streaming through the window. *Why couldn't I have a buddy like that?* Wendy thought rebelliously.

A few minutes later she was ashamed of her unkind thoughts as Mr. Douglas spoke to them very earnestly. He reminded them that the Lord Jesus loved their buddies just as much as He loved them. He told them that Jesus had commanded us to love one another just like He loved us.

As Mr. Douglas dismissed them with a short prayer, Wendy determined in her heart that she *would* love Maggie. Turning to the girl beside her, Wendy smiled warmly as she said, "Hey, Maggie. Come and meet my friend Susan. Then we'll go over to your cabin."

Wendy's effort was rewarded by seeing the anxious look fade from Maggie's eyes as she mumbled, "OK." Then getting awkwardly to her feet, she followed Wendy toward the door.

When Wendy and Maggie got outside, they found Susan and Cheryl waiting for them. The

Maggie up quickly. And she said there were some clothes on hand that were kept for anyone who needed them. Wendy left Maggie in Miss Ardill's care and ran across to the play field to see if she could find Brian.

Brian and Randy were sitting under a tree talking. "What's wrong?" Wendy asked as she saw their serious faces. "I thought you would be playing ball."

Brian gave a quick look around, then he said, "Something has happened, Wendy. Sit down and I'll tell you about it."

"Is it Pete?" Wendy asked, slipping down on the grass beside them. "I hope he isn't giving you trouble, Brian."

"Shh! Not so loud," Brian said in a low voice. Then he continued, "Pete is OK—I *think*. But when we first went to his cabin and I was helping him unpack, he told me he didn't have any spending money. He said his 'old man'— that's what he calls his father—wouldn't give him any. He sounded real angry about it. So I went to my cabin to get a quarter to give him.

"But when I got back, Pete wasn't in his cabin. The only one there was a younger boy called Bobby. He was sitting on his bed near Pete's, and he was crying."

"Was he homesick?" Wendy asked, sympathy in her voice.

Brian shook his head. "No, he was crying because he had come to get the money that he had left in his suitcase and he said a whole dollar was missing."

"Oh," Wendy said, her eyes wide. "Do you think Pete took the money, Brian?"

"It looks like it," Randy put in. "But we have to be *sure* before we say anything."

"How can you be sure?" Wendy asked. "It could be any one of the other boys in the cabin. Remember what Mr. Douglas said about trying to help our camp buddy and loving him and everything. You won't be able to do that, Brian, if you doubt Pete right from the start."

"I know, Wendy," Brian answered, wrinkling his brow in a worried frown. "And I was just thinking of our golden verse and wondering if Jesus would want me to go and tell our counselor, Mr. Kenneth. The trouble is that I don't think Pete is a Christian by the way he talked. He used some bad words and he said something about not liking the Bible lessons and having to memorize verses. So I'm afraid if I tell Mr. Kenneth now, Pete will be mad at me and I won't be able to help him become a Christian."

"You *can't* tell Mr. Kenneth yet, Brian," Wendy insisted. "You don't have any proof."

"I have more than you think," Brian lowered his voice to a whisper as some kids were passing by. "Just a few minutes ago, I saw Pete, and he was eating a big double-dip ice cream cone. So where did he get the money to buy it? That's what we've got to find out!"

"And that's not all," Randy added. "While Brian was getting his money, I ran across to the kitchen for a minute. On my way back I saw Pete dash out of his cabin straight toward the canteen. Biff Frankson was standing there waiting for him, and they went into the canteen together. I know Biff, and he isn't a good guy to have for a friend. He visits a family down our street in the summertime, and the kids there are always in trouble when Biff is around."

Just then the supper bell rang. Brian jumped to his feet. "We'd better hurry and get in line," he said. "See me after breakfast tomorrow, Wendy. Maybe we will know something more by then."

11

The Strange Old Man

When breakfast was over the next morning, Wendy and Susan hurried down toward the beach where Brian and Randy were waiting for them. Wendy had told Susan all about the stolen money, and Susan was just as eager as Wendy to hear more about it.

Wendy and Susan raced over to where the boys were standing. "Did you find out anything more?" Wendy asked breathlessly.

Brian shook his head. "Not very much. I did ask Pete where he got the ice cream cone I saw him eating. But he just clammed up and wouldn't tell me a thing."

"Too bad," Susan said. "What are you going to do now?"

"We don't know yet," Brian answered slowly.

"We were trying to figure out something that Joey said. You tell them, Randy."

"Well, Joey is my buddy, you know," Randy began. "And his bed is next to mine. This morning when we were all supposed to be reading our Bibles, I looked up and saw that Joey had an open comic book on top of his Bible. He saw me looking at him, so he put it away quickly. On the way to breakfast I asked him if he was a Christian. He said he was and that he really did love the Bible. But the comic book was a new one and very exciting and he couldn't wait to finish it. So I asked him if he had brought it from home and do you know what he said?"

"What?" the girls asked in the same breath.

"He told me that Pete had sold it to him yesterday," Randy answered. "Brian and I can't understand where Pete got it. And Joey said that Pete sold some comics to a lot of other kids, too."

"If Pete did that, then he would have plenty of money for an ice cream cone," Wendy said thoughtfully as she smoothed back the dark hair from her forehead. "But where did he get the comic books?"

"There aren't any in the canteen," Brian told them. "We looked just now."

"Did Bobby tell his counselor about the stolen money?" Wendy asked.

"Yes, he did. And Bobby said that his counselor talked to them last night. He told them that the stolen money would be a mark against their whole cabin unless someone owned up to it and made things right. But so far no one has done so," Brian answered.

Just then the bell rang for the morning chapel hour, and the four of them rushed off toward their cabins to get their Bibles.

"Do you think we should check on Maggie and Cheryl?" Susan asked, stopping at Cabin 8 while the other children surged past them.

"I suppose we should this time," Wendy agreed. "But after this I don't think it will be necessary."

They found Cheryl looking very cross as two of her cabin mates stood over her. They were insisting that she clear off her bed before leaving. "You are going to make our cabin lose points if you leave your bed in a mess like this," Tracey Atkins told Cheryl loudly. "And it isn't fair!"

Susan put down her Bible. "I'm Cheryl's buddy, and I will help her clean up. You girls can go on to the meeting."

The girls watched for a minute as Susan

opened up Cheryl's suitcase and began to take
the things off the bed and put them into the suitcase as quickly as she could. Then, satisfied that
Susan meant what she said, they ran out of the
cabin.

"Oh, what pretty beads!" Susan exclaimed, as
she held up a pair of blue and white beads before
putting them into the suitcase.

Cheryl's mouth, which had been pouting,
turned up in a smile. "I like them, too. I bought
them just last night from a boy. I think his name is
Pete Brown. He had a lot to sell, but I thought
those were the prettiest."

Wendy had started toward Maggie's bed, but at
Cheryl's words, Wendy turned and stared at Susan. Then, motioning for Susan not to say anything, Wendy went on down the aisle.

She found Maggie sitting on her bed, looking
half asleep. "Oh, Maggie, do hurry!" Wendy
exclaimed, "or we'll all be late."

"Do I have to go?" Maggie asked with a yawn.

"Yes, of course. Didn't Miss Ardill tell you that?"

"Ummm," Maggie answered, rising and stretching lazily. "But I am so sleepy. I thought I'd go back
to sleep after they all cleared out."

"You can't do that," Wendy told her, taking

Maggie's hand and half tugging her along. "I'd think you would *want* to obey Miss Ardill after she gave you those nice clothes you showed me last night. That striped top looks great with those jeans, Maggie. It makes you look a lot slimmer."

"Does it?" Maggie looked pleased, and she began to move along more quickly.

Once outside, the four girls broke into a run and made it to the main building just before the doors were closed. Anyone coming later would be allowed in but a point would be deducted from his record card.

The happy singing and cheerful tone of the whole meeting soon roused Maggie from her sleepiness and took away the sullen look from Cheryl's face. Wendy and Susan looked at each other and smiled as they saw the deep interest in the faces of their camp buddies as Mr. Douglas got up to speak.

First Mr. Douglas showed them a beautiful Bible. "There will be a Bible like this for the girl with the highest points and one for the boy with the highest points," he told them. "By the way some of you are starting out, I'm sure we are going to have some stiff competition. So keep on trying."

Wendy's heart was fluttering with excitement. "I

must win that Bible," she told herself. "Wouldn't Granny be pleased! And I do need one." She looked down at the small, worn Bible in her hand. It was an old one that her cousin Janice had given her.

Just then Wendy glanced at Susan and was startled to see a big tear roll down her friend's cheek. Wendy looked away at once, an uneasy feeling growing inside her. Susan wanted that Bible too. She wanted it so much it even made her cry. And she certainly needed one. All she had was an old one of her mother's. The back was loose and many of the pages were torn and parts of some chapters were missing completely.

"We can't both win it," Wendy thought. "But I have just as much right to try for it as Susan has. And I will, too," she promised herself stubbornly.

"That ye might walk worthy of the Lord unto all pleasing—" The words hammered their way into Wendy's tangled thoughts as Mr. Douglas had the children repeat the golden verse over and over again. Then he gave them a little talk explaining that sometimes we had to choose between pleasing ourselves and pleasing the Lord Jesus. Wendy listened, but there seemed to be a hard lump deep inside her that did not want to go away.

After the meeting, the girls were told it was their time for swimming. They all dashed for their swim suits and were soon shouting and laughing as they plunged into the cool water of the lake.

Wendy was surprised to see that Maggie was an excellent swimmer. Wendy watched in silence for a few minutes. Then she clapped her hands and called out, "Hey, Maggie, where did you learn to swim like that?" The other girls stopped to watch. Maggie was swimming, floating, and diving under the water with almost unbelievable ease and grace.

"Say, that's great! Who taught you to swim like that, Maggie?" Miss Ardill asked as she joined the group.

"Aw," Maggie said, growing embarrassed at all the attention. "We live near a lake, and my daddy taught me to swim when I was a baby, almost. It's nothing."

"It's a great accomplishment, Maggie," Miss Ardill assured her. "Would you be willing to help me teach some of the younger ones during part of your swimming period each day?"

"Sure, if you want me to," Maggie answered. Her eyes were glowing in spite of her embarrassment. It made Wendy feel happy just to look at her.

"Maggie is beginning to grow," she thought. Then a wistful feeling swelled up in Wendy's heart. "I want to grow too, Lord Jesus," she prayed. "Please help me."

The next day passed quietly with special Sunday programs that all the children enjoyed. Maggie looked nice in a candy-striped dress Miss Ardill had found for her. And ever since the swimming triumph, Maggie had been making friends with others in her cabin. But Cheryl seemed quiet and unhappy. Wendy asked Susan about it when they went for a walk by themselves that afternoon.

"It's because of what happened yesterday just before supper," Susan explained. "I heard someone crying in cabin 8, and when I asked some girls who it was, they giggled and said it was the 'princess' crying for her mommy. So I went in and found Cheryl sobbing and saying she wanted to go home. I couldn't tell Miss Ardill because she had gone for a walk with some of the girls. But Cheryl finally told me that because of her pretty clothes, the other girls teased her and called her 'princess.' She said that no one liked her or would play with her and she wanted to phone for her mother to come and get her."

"I'm not surprised that the kids are teasing her,"

Wendy said. "Cheryl is too proud of her clothes and can talk of nothing else."

Susan's blue eyes were troubled as she nodded. "I know, Wendy. But Cheryl is the only child in her family. She told me that her mother won't let her wear jeans to school and will only let her play with rich kids. It was her daddy who heard about this camp and insisted on sending her here. I feel sorry for her, because I think she would really like to be able to play with the other kids and have fun but she doesn't know how. At first I envied her with all those pretty dresses, but I don't now."

"I know!" Wendy suddenly exclaimed. "Let's ask Miss Ardill to find some jeans and tops for Cheryl. If Cheryl will wear them, she will soon mix in with the other kids and won't act like a dressed-up doll."

"What would her mother say?" Susan asked doubtfully.

"Her daddy sent her here, didn't he?" Wendy declared. "I bet he was getting tired of a 'princess' for a daughter and would like a real girl for a change."

Susan laughed. "I guess maybe he would. I'll talk to Cheryl about it the first chance I get."

Wendy and Susan had been following a path

that circled the inside boundary of the camp grounds. They were nearing the entrance gates when they were both startled by a loud "Psst!" A movement in the bushes just ahead of them showed Brian and Randy crouching down and motioning them to do the same. Ducking low, the girls ran over to the bush and kneeled down beside the boys.

"What is it?" Wendy whispered fearfully.

"Shh, look over there by the gate," Brian murmured.

The girls peeked through the bushes. They saw an old man with a violin by his side. He was sitting near the entrance to the camp grounds. Pete was squatting beside him, hurriedly stuffing into his pockets the things the old man was handing to him. The last thing the man gave him looked like a roll of papers. Pete stuck it inside his jacket and with a wave of his hand, he ran back into the camp grounds and headed in the direction of his cabin.

"W-who is that old man?" Susan's voice trembled with excitement.

Randy shook his head, puzzled. "I don't know," he said, "but I think—"

"You think that Mr. Douglas should know about

this, don't you?" Brian interrupted. "Well, so do I. And it's nearly time for supper, so we'll have to make a dash for it if we want to catch Mr. Douglas before he leaves his cabin. Come on."

The boys were off before the girls had a chance to ask any more questions. "Oh," Wendy sighed. "I hope Pete won't get into trouble and have to go home, 'cause I don't think he has taken the Lord Jesus as his Savior yet."

"Maybe he will when Mr. Douglas talks to him," Susan said hopefully as they got to their feet and started on a run toward the dining hall.

12

The Leather Wallet

It was not until the next morning, just before the regular Bible lesson, that Brian and Randy were able to tell Wendy and Susan what had happened. They had been looking for each other and had finally met in one corner of the main building. A number of the boys and girls had already gathered around the piano near the front and were singing some of the camp songs.

"We didn't get to see Mr. Douglas," Brian said in a low voice as the girls joined them. "We asked Mr. Kenneth if he knew where Mr. Douglas was, and he told us that Mr. Douglas had been called away on an important matter and would not get back until just before the meeting this morning."

"So that was why we didn't see him here last night," Wendy said. "We were worried because we didn't see him or you. Where were you?"

"Well, when we couldn't find Mr. Douglas, we went ahead and told Mr. Kenneth all about everything. He looked real serious and said he would tell Mr. Douglas the first chance he got this morning. He told us that the old man is Mr. O'Patrick, and they have never had any trouble with him before. Guess he often has been allowed to come and play his violin for the kids. Mr. Kenneth asked us so many questions that we were late for the meeting and sat way back in the corner. That's why you didn't see us," Brian finished.

"Oh," Susan said. "Did they take points off for being late?"

"No," Randy answered with a grin. "Mr. Kenneth told them that we were talking with him, and not to dock us, so they didn't."

"I hope Mr. Douglas won't want to see us right after the Bible lesson," Brian said a bit anxiously. "It will cut into our craft period, and I need every minute I can get to finish my wallet. You should see it, Wendy. I'm making it for Daddy, and I think he will like it."

"Like it!" Randy exclaimed. "I should *say* he will

like it. It's great! None of the rest of us have a chance for the craft prize, I can tell you that."

Wendy's eyes were sparkling as she said, "I'm so glad, Brian. And I think it will make Daddy happy even if you don't win a prize." Then remembering her father's unhappy face, she added softly to Brian, "And Daddy needs something to make him happy, you know he does."

Just then the bell rang, and as the other two moved away, Brian said to Wendy, "Listen, Wendy. I'm putting the words *God loves you* on the back of the wallet. Do you think that will help Daddy?"

"Oh, yes," Wendy answered. "And I'm making a jewelry box for Mother. Maybe I could write out a Bible verse and put it in the box."

"Good idea," Brian agreed as they joined the others, and the meeting began.

Later that morning, during craft time, Miss Marion came over to where Wendy and Susan were busily working. "Girls," she said, "we are out of white thread. I know you hate to miss any of your craft time, but I would be grateful if you would run to the store for me."

"Sure, Miss Marion," Wendy and Susan answered, putting down their work and standing up.

"Is it that little store just down a piece from the gate?" Wendy asked.

"Yes, that's it. I'll give you a note to the man who owns the store, and he will give you the thread. If you hurry, it will take just a few minutes."

The girls started off on a run. They sped out the gate and down the road to the store. They stopped at the partly-opened door to catch their breath and were startled to hear someone inside the store mention Camp Good Hope.

"Yes," a man's voice was saying, "we started missing things the day that camp opened. Children's beads and pens and comic books and things like that. And the man who runs a little store down at the crossroads told me he was having the same trouble. Funny thing though," the voice went on, "we don't have very many kids coming in here from the camp. But believe me, we are sure keeping our eyes on those who do."

Wendy and Susan stared at each other, their eyes round with fright. "Let's go back," Susan whispered.

Wendy grabbed Susan's arm. "We can't! We're not going to steal anything. Come on!" Setting her chin firmly, Wendy pushed the half-opened door wide and led the way into the store.

Just then a group of older boys brushed past them and headed toward the man behind the counter. Wendy looked toward the side counter and saw a pleasant lady there. The lady finished waiting on a customer and then turned to Wendy and asked what she wanted.

Wendy silently handed her the note and, although the woman glanced at them keenly, she didn't say anything. She gave them the thread, and with a quick "thank you," Wendy and Susan hurried out of the store.

The girls ran all the way back to the craft room without speaking. At the door Wendy said, "We only have a few more minutes of crafts, and then we'll go and tell Mr. Douglas. Okay?"

Susan nodded as they went into the craft room and gave Miss Marion the thread.

As soon as their craft period was over, Wendy and Susan hurried to Mr. Douglas's cabin and knocked on the door. Mr. Douglas opened the door and led them into the room. The girls were surprised to see Brian and Randy and Mr. Kenneth there.

Mr. Douglas smiled kindly at the two girls. "I can tell by your flushed cheeks and bright eyes that you have something exciting to tell me," he said.

"But do you think you could talk to my wife in the other room while we finish our serious discussion with these young fellows here?"

"But it's about the same thing," Wendy blurted out. "We were sent over to the store by Miss Marion and the man there said he started missing things like beads and comic books and pens the day camp started. He is keeping watch on all the kids from camp 'cause he thinks we are doing the stealing."

Mr. Douglas's face took on a troubled look. "Did you know about this before?" he asked.

"Yes," Brian put in. "Wendy is my sister and that's her friend Susan. They know all about Biff and Pete and everything."

When Mr. Douglas heard that, he asked the girls to sit down and tell him everything they had heard. He asked a number of questions. Then he sighed heavily as he rose to his feet. "I'm very sorry about all this," he told the children. "But we are thankful you told us before it went on any longer. Please don't say anything to the other campers about it. We will attend to everything this afternoon and make an announcement tonight so that all this business will come to an end." After thanking them again, he told them they could go.

Once outside, Brian exclaimed, "Say! you girls sure came just at the right moment."

"Why?" Susan asked. "Didn't Mr. Douglas believe you?"

"Oh, yes, he believed us all right," Randy put in. "But he has known Mr. O'Patrick for quite awhile, and he thought that Mr. O'Patrick must be buying the things up cheaply and trying to make a little bit of money out of the campers. He didn't think that anything as bad as *stealing* was going on."

Brian didn't look at the others as he said, "Guess this will finish me with Pete. He will think all Christians are tattle-tales, and he won't even want to be my buddy anymore."

Wendy could tell by Brian's voice that he was feeling all chokey inside. "We'll all pray for Pete," she said. "We'll pray real hard. The Lord Jesus can change Pete before camp is over."

"Sure," Randy encouraged. "We have three full days yet before we have to go home. A whole lot could happen in that time."

That evening when Mr. Douglas stood up to talk to them, there was a sudden hush as he said, "I have something very sad to tell you tonight." Then he went ahead and told them that the old man who had played the violin for them had been guilty of stealing some things and selling them to two of the boys at the camp. But since the boys did not know the things were stolen, they would only be punished for going off bounds. The boys admitted that they had waited till no one else was around, and then left the grounds. They secretly received the things from Mr. O'Patrick. Then they sold them to their camp companions. The very fact that the boys did it secretly showed that they knew they were doing wrong. The boys would be punished by not being allowed to go swimming for the remainder of the camp.

"Because this is Mr. O'Patrick's first offense, and since he is an old man, the police have asked him only to pay for the things he has stolen. Mr. O'Patrick has paid for them, and the storekeepers have agreed not to press charges. They told me that you children may keep the things you have bought. I hope you will all pray for Mr. O'Patrick. We would like to see him take the Lord as his Savior." Mr. Douglas paused for a minute, then he asked, "Does anyone here have anything to say about all this?"

The room was very still as Mr. Douglas waited. Then Joey jumped up and said, "I'm sorry that I bought some of those comics. They weren't the funny kind. They were the kind that give you bad thoughts in your mind. And— and— after I read them I didn't feel like reading my Bible. I threw them in the fire today. I don't want to read that kind any more 'cause our golden verse tells us to do the things that will please Jesus. And I just know the Lord Jesus wouldn't read that stuff."

"You have made a wise decision, Joey," Mr. Douglas commended him. "Stick to it."

Just then Cheryl stood up and said in a trembly voice, "I bought some beads with the money my daddy gave me for the Sunday offering. And I'm— I'm— sorry." She began to sob as she sat down. Miss Ardill went over and put an arm around her.

Mr. Douglas cleared his throat as he said, "Sin has far-reaching effects, boys and girls. It is not something we can play with." Then he talked to them quietly about how a seemingly little sin can grow and spread until many, many people are harmed by it. After Mr. Douglas had finished speaking to them, a number of boys and girls stayed behind to talk to their counselors. The rest went to their cabins and settled down more quickly than usual.

It wasn't until the next afternoon that Wendy had a chance to talk to Brian. He came running toward her, his face white and full of misery. "Wendy," he whispered, "my wallet is ruined. Completely ruined."

A sick, numb feeling filled Wendy's heart as she looked at her brother. "Oh, Brian, what happened?" she asked. "Did you cut it by mistake?"

"*Me* cut it?" he almost yelled. "I didn't do it. It was fine when I put it away yesterday. But today when we went to crafts, I found that someone had cut it. It's all jagged around the edge. It's a mess! And I'm sure it was Pete who did it, because I can tell he is still mad at me. 'Love your buddy.' Huh! Who could love a buddy that would do a thing like that?"

13

The Hornet's Nest

That night Wendy found it hard to go to sleep. Brian had told her that Mr. Kenneth had promised to help fix the wallet during their next craft period. But Brian had not been very hopeful about it. And he was still angry at Pete.

Wendy sighed and tried to get her mind on happier thoughts. If only she could win that prize Bible, how pleased Granny would be. One of the counselors had told Wendy and Susan that five girls were at the top of the list as far as points were concerned and Wendy and Susan were two of them. But they could not *all* win the Bible.

Wendy tossed uneasily as she thought of how much Susan wanted to win the Bible. And Susan really needed that Bible. With a jerk, Wendy turned her hot pillow over and, closing her eyes, she finally dropped into a troubled sleep.

Before breakfast the next morning, Cheryl came skipping over to where Wendy and Susan were hanging out their towels to dry. "Something good happened last night," she told them. "Miss Ardill talked to me, and I asked the Lord Jesus to be my Savior. I've never been so happy before— never!" Her blue eyes were shining, and her whole face was alive with happiness.

"Oh, Cheryl, I'm so glad," Susan said. "I've been praying that you would do that."

"And now you have your name in Jesus' book of life," Wendy told her. At Cheryl's puzzled look, Wendy explained to her about the Lamb's book of life. She was still answering Cheryl's questions when the breakfast bell rang, and they ran to get in line.

At the table, Wendy whispered to Susan, "Cheryl looks cute in those jeans and top. Has she made any new friends yet?"

Susan nodded. "Yes, I saw her playing with some kids yesterday. And now that she has the Lord Jesus to help her, I think she will begin to grow like Jesus wants us to. Don't you think so too?"

Wendy murmured a reply as a little stab of envy went through her. "Everyone is growing but me," she thought. "I wish I could grow too. Maybe I would if I wasn't so selfish in wanting to win that Bible." But she quickly pushed the thought away and began to talk to the girl across the table from her.

After breakfast, instead of waiting for Susan, Wendy slipped away to find Brian. He was still unhappy about his wallet, but he told Wendy that he had asked Jesus to help him forgive Pete. "I don't feel mad at Pete any more," Brian said. "I don't think I love him though—at least not very much," he added honestly.

"Maybe you will be able to after awhile," Wendy encouraged him. "Do you still think he took Bobby's money?"

"I don't know." Brian skipped a stone on the water as they stood beside the lake. "But whoever took it must have felt sorry. Because Bobby told me that he found a dollar on top of the clothes in his suitcase yesterday."

"Oh, good. I'm glad he got his money back." Wendy paused, then went on, "It isn't easy to grow to be more like the Lord Jesus, is it, Brian?"

A dull red crept up in Brian's face. "Do you

mean because I got so mad at Pete last night?
I—"

"No, I wasn't thinking of that," Wendy interrupted. *"You* are growing, Brian. Because you
have already asked Jesus to help you forgive Pete.
I'm the one that isn't growing. I want to. I really do.
But I don't think I am."

"Maybe Jesus can see that you are growing inside, Wendy," Brian comforted her. "Say! Look at
the foam on those waves. Doesn't it bubble up
just like soap suds?"

"Soap suds!" Wendy's hand flew to her mouth
and her eyes grew wide as she stared at her
brother. "Oh, it was my turn to help with the
dishes and I forgot all about it. Now I'll lose a point."
With a groan Wendy turned and fled up the path
toward the kitchen.

At the kitchen door Wendy met Susan coming
out. "I— I— forgot," Wendy gasped. "Did they call
my name?"

Susan put her arm through Wendy's and led
her away from the kitchen. "Yes, they called your
name, Wendy. But I said I would change with you.
I've just finished. You can do it in my place tomorrow."

"Thanks a million, Susan," Wendy gulped. "Do

you think it's all right? I would have lost a point, you know, if you hadn't taken my place."

"Of course it's all right. The kids are changing with each other all the time. The ladies in the kitchen don't mind as long as someone takes our place."

Just then the bell rang for the morning Bible lessons. The girls got their Bibles and followed the crowd to the main building. "I hope Mr. Douglas doesn't ask me for the golden verse today," Susan whispered nervously. "I didn't get time to go over it this morning."

"I'm sorry, Susan. It's all my fault that you didn't get time to study the verse," Wendy said. "I hope he won't ask you today."

But when Mr. Douglas began to call on different ones to say the verse, Susan's name was the second on the list. Susan got as far as, "being fruitful in every good work—," then she stopped. Wendy longed to prompt her but that was against the rules.

Dear Lord Jesus, please help Susan to remember, Wendy prayed in her heart. Just when Mr. Douglas started to tell her to sit down, Susan remembered the words and finished the verse with a rush.

"Good for you," Wendy whispered as Susan wiped the beads of perspiration from her face and gave Wendy a shaky smile. Wendy thought to herself, *Susan is the most unselfish person in the world. And I'm the most selfish. I don't want to be like that. I've got to do something about it. But what?*

Wendy saw Brian a few minutes after craft period and he told her with a big smile that Mr. Kenneth had fixed his wallet. He had brought a little machine and had made a zig-zag pattern over the place where they had added the new piece. "Of course I can't win a prize with it because Mr. Kenneth did the sewing and it wasn't all my work. But I don't mind—as long as Daddy likes it," Brian said. "Now, I've got to hurry. The boys are all going on a hike. Bye," he called over his shoulder as he ran off.

The girls practiced most of the afternoon for the final sports events they were to have the next day. In one race Linda Sooter slyly tried to trip Wendy as she raced past her. Wendy felt the angry tears sting her eyes but suddenly the golden verse flashed into her mind. *"That you might walk worthy of the Lord unto all pleasing."* Wendy fought back her tears and ran on. Later she saw Linda watching her, but she didn't say anything.

It was nearly supper time when the boys got back from their hike. Brian and Randy came over to where Susan and Wendy were sitting on the steps of the main building.

The boys were wild with excitement and began at once to tell the two girls all that had happened on the hike. They said that Biff and Pete had bothered them and said mean things to them— that they had talked just loud enough so the counselor could not hear, but the other kids could.

Finally, Biff and Pete got tired of that and started to lag behind. Brian had looked around just in time to see them turn off the path and enter the woods. He thought they were just being smart and would soon return to the path. But when they didn't, Brian had told Mr. Kenneth. So they had all turned back, and Mr. Roberts had taken the rest of the boys back to camp while Mr. Kenneth and Brian and Randy had gone into the woods to look for the boys.

"We found Pete quite a long way from the path. He was lying on the ground and man, was he in bad shape!" Brian said.

Wendy and Brian and the Hurt Puppy

"What happened to him?" the girls asked. "And where was Biff?"

"Pete told us that he had been getting fed up with the things Biff was doing, and that he was ashamed of his part in it too. So he had told Biff he was through and that he was going back and own up to what he had done and try to make things right. That made Biff so mad he started hitting Pete. In their fight, Biff knocked Pete over backwards and he landed against a hornet's nest hanging in the bush behind him."

"Oh, how terrible," Wendy exclaimed with a shiver. "Did he get stung a lot?"

"You bet he did," Randy said. "His face and hands were swollen. He felt so bad he could hardly walk. We helped him back to camp and left him with the nurse. Mr. Kenneth went further into the woods to look for Biff. You see, when Pete showed him the direction Biff had gone, Mr. Kenneth knew that Biff was headed the wrong way. Biff had said he would go to get help, but he must have gotten lost because Mr. Kenneth still isn't back."

"But listen to this," Brian said triumphantly. "Pete told me he was sorry for taking Bobby's money and cutting my wallet. He asked me to

forgive him. Of course, I did. He asked the Lord
Jesus to forgive him too, and to be his Savior. Isn't
that great? Now I have a real camp buddy." Brian's
voice was full of satisfaction and Wendy was glad
to see the happy look back on his face.

"I sure hope they find Biff soon. He needs
Jesus, too," Randy said. "He really, really does."

14

Growing At Last

The next morning the whole place was astir with noise and excitement. It was the children's last full day at camp. Some of the parents were coming for the program that afternoon. They would take their children home with them after the program was over. The remaining campers would be taken home by bus the following morning.

On their way to the morning Bible lesson, Wendy and Susan shouted for Maggie and Cheryl to hurry. Soon their two buddies came scurrying out of cabin 8 and joined them.

"I've got all my things packed, except for the dress I'll be wearing home," Cheryl told them. "I can hardly wait for my mother and daddy to come."

"I hope your mother won't mind when she sees you wearing jeans," Susan said, a bit troubled.

"I wrote and told her, so she will be used to the idea by now." Cheryl gave a little giggle as she skipped along beside them. "I know my daddy won't mind. He always said I should get out and play with the other kids on our street. I hope I can too. It will be fun. And I want to tell the kids about the Lord Jesus and all the things I've learned here at camp."

"I wish my mother and daddy would come, but I don't think there is much chance that they will take time off from their work," Wendy said with a sigh.

"My parents are coming. Would you like to meet them?" Maggie asked shyly.

"Of course I would, Maggie." Wendy linked her arm in Maggie's as she spoke. "You're my camp buddy, and I want you to write to me. Will you?"

Maggie nodded wordlessly, but she looked at Wendy with shining eyes. As Wendy smiled back at her, she thought to herself, "Maggie has changed a lot in just one week. She keeps herself clean too, now that she has enough clothes."

The girls stopped their chatter as they entered the main building and settled down for the Bible lesson.

Mr. Douglas told them that Biff had been found

late the night before. He said that Biff was unharmed but was too worn out to attend the morning class. Then Mr. Douglas went on to explain that when we disobey, we not only bring trouble upon ourselves, but often our friends and family have to suffer too.

"I'm glad to say," Mr. Douglas smiled kindly as he continued, "yesterday's trouble has caused one boy to change his ways. Pete, do you want to come up and tell us about it?"

Pete made his way slowly toward the front. "I don't know what to say— I— uh—," he paused. Then running his fingers through his hair, he struggled on, "I'm sorry about taking Bobby's money. I've already paid him back and asked him to forgive me.

"And I'm sure sorry I cut Brian's wallet. I— I— guess I was mad at Brian because I could see he was trying to please Jesus. I kept telling myself that I wasn't going to read the Bible and learn the verses and all that stuff. Down inside me though, I felt as mean and miserable as a dog with a sore paw. So I told Biff I was going to come back and own up to everything. He got mad and we had a fight and I got stung with hornets. But when Brian and Randy were helping me home, I told Brian I was sorry. He forgave me and showed me how I could ask Jesus to forgive me and be my Savior. So I— I— did. And— well— I guess that's all."

"Thank you, Pete," Mr. Douglas said. "We are all very glad that you have taken the Lord Jesus as your Savior. You will find it is the only way you can be truly happy."

Mr. Douglas then spoke briefly but with deep feeling on the sin of disobedience. When he had finished, the room was very still. Mr. Douglas looked at the boys and girls in silence for a minute, then he said, "If anyone wants to stay and speak to your counselor, you may do so. The rest of you are dismissed."

Once outside, Brian and Randy came over to where Susan and Wendy were standing. Cheryl and Maggie came running up to them and begged Wendy and Susan to come and meet their parents who had just arrived.

Later, after lunch and a short rest period, the children all gathered in the playing field for the final races and games.

As Wendy and Susan were practicing the three-legged race before the games began, Wendy stopped and untied the cloth from her leg. "You should do this race with someone else, Susan. I just can't get started right, and I always hold you back."

"That's all right, Wendy," Susan said cheerfully. "We'll do our best, even if we don't win."

Wendy thought to herself, *If Susan could win this race, she would be sure to get the prize Bible.* Suddenly an idea hit her—hard. She looked over to where Linda Sooter and a girl named Sally were practicing the same race. Linda seemed to be dragging Sally half the time.

Wendy sprinted across the field and grabbed Linda's arm. "Linda," she said urgently, "come here a minute. I want to ask you something."

Linda gave Wendy a suspicious look. Then she followed her to a spot where they could be by themselves. "Listen," Wendy said. "I can't do the three-legged race any better than Sally can. But you and Susan are both good at it. You can win it. I know you can. Will you be Susan's partner and let me be Sally's?"

Linda gave her an unbelieving stare. "Are you trying to trick me, Wendy Tompson?" she demanded.

"Trick you!" Wendy exclaimed. "I'm trying to help you and Susan win first in that race. I know you can do it! Come on and try it out."

Susan protested when she heard what Wendy wanted. But Wendy would not listen. Hurriedly she tied Linda's and Susan's legs together and told them to practice. Then she and Sally practiced together.

Just then the whistle blew, and the girls lined up for the three-legged race. Susan and Linda were in the first group, and at the sound of the whistle they were off like a flash. Wendy and Sally cheered them on, and Wendy screamed with delight when she saw Susan and Linda win first place.

Wendy and Sally tried in the next group but did not get very far before they stumbled and were out of the race.

"Oh, Wendy," Susan said unhappily. "I'm sorry you didn't make it. Now I'm ahead of you in points. Did you know there were three points for first in this race?"

"Yes, but that's all right," replied Wendy. "I'm glad you won. Thanks, Linda," Wendy smiled at Linda who was still looking a bit surprised. "You and Susan sure made a good team in that race."

"Thanks for asking me," Linda said as she ran off.

"Wendy and Susan, come quickly," Brian gasped as he trotted up to them. "Mother and

Daddy have come. So have Randy's parents. Your mother is here too, Susan. And someone else, Wendy. Come and see."

The girls followed Brian through the crowd to where a group of parents and other visitors were sitting watching the sports. Wendy threw her arms around her mother and gave her father a big hug. Then she said "Hello" to Mrs. Blake.

"What about me, Wendy?" someone called. And there, sitting in a chair, her eyes twinkling, was Granny.

"Oh, Granny," Wendy's voice rose in a squeak of surprise. "I'm so glad, glad, glad you are here." She flung her arms around Granny in a warm hug.

The rest of the afternoon passed like a dream to Wendy. After the sports were over, refreshments were served to the visitors. Then the prizes were given out. Wendy and Brian told their parents and Granny the names of those who won the prizes. They cheered when Joey won the sports prize and Jim Johnson the craft prize for the boys. When they heard that the prize cabin was cabin 8, Wendy began to tell Granny about Maggie and Cheryl.

Just then Mr. Douglas got up with the prize

Bibles in his hand. A sudden hush settled over the excited children.

"We have had a splendid group of boys and girls at camp this year," Mr. Douglas said. "Among the girls it was a very close race. But the girl with the highest number of points is—Miss Susan Blake."

Wendy heaved a big sigh of relief as she saw Susan go forward and receive the Bible. "I wanted to win it, Granny," Wendy whispered, with her head on Granny's shoulder. "But Susan needed it more than I did. And she really earned it too."

Mr. Douglas had called up a boy to receive the prize Bible for the boys. Wendy did not know him very well. "He's a great guy," Brian assured them, "and he wanted that Bible a lot. I know he did."

"Now," Mr. Douglas continued. "We are starting something new this year. We have a list of boys and girls who have been outstanding in their cooperation, obedience, and helpfulness to their camp buddies. We feel that they have made a real contribution to the success of the camp. We want to give each of them a small reward."

As the names were called, Wendy was delighted to hear Brian's and Randy's and Susan's names. Then her heart leaped as she heard her own name called. She went forward and gazed with wonder at the lovely little picture that was given to her. The picture was of a white-haired woman with an open Bible on her lap. Two children, a boy and a girl, were sitting at her knee as if listening to a story from the Bible. Underneath the picture were the words from Psalm 119:11, "Thy word have I hid in mine heart, that I might not sin against thee."

Wendy and Brian ran back to show their pictures to their parents and Granny. Then they had to hurry and pack and say good-bye to all their friends. It seemed hard to believe that camp was over.

It was not until they were at home the next evening that they were able to tell Granny all the other things about camp that they wanted her to know.

Brian told her all about his wallet. "Daddy was so pleased when I gave it to him. He didn't mind that it had been cut. He told me he thought it was well done and he was proud of me."

"Mommy liked the little box I gave her," Wendy said, smiling. "And she read the verse I put inside it too. It was one I learned at camp."

"I learned a lot of new verses too. Camp sure was great," Brian said with a contented sigh.

"The hardest part of all was learning to grow more like Jesus," Wendy said. "I could see Brian growing. And I wanted to grow too."

"Sometimes I didn't grow very fast," Brian said with a shake of his head. "Remember how mad I got at my buddy and I felt real mean about him inside, too."

"Growing takes time," Granny told them. "But a boy who helped his buddy when he was in trouble, and then forgave that buddy freely, and even showed him how to take the Lord Jesus as his Savior— well, I feel sure that boy was learning to grow.

"And it seems to me that a girl who helps her buddy gain confidence in herself and takes time to win that buddy's friendship, is a girl who is growing. And only a girl who is learning to grow to be like Jesus can be happy to see her friend win a prize that she herself wanted."

"Oh, thank you, Granny," Wendy said. "I want to keep on growing every day, even if it is hard."

"Me too," Brian echoed. Then, with a sleepy "Good-night," the children went upstairs to bed.

Moody Press, a ministry of the Moody Bible Institute, is designed for education, evangelization, and edification. If we may assist you in knowing more about Christ and the Christian life, please write us without obligation: Moody Press, c/o MLM, Chicago, Illinois 60610.